For you Zu Zu, you are my reason.

For information about this title or to order other books and/or electronic media,

please contact the publisher:

thezmh.com

Zou Zou Media House c/o Woolcock Patton, LLC

488 Schooley's Mountain Road, Bldg 1A

Hackettstown, NJ 07840

Printed in the United States of America

First Edition: May 2020

Publisher's Cataloging-in-Publication Data

Names: Campbell, Valene, author.

Title: The amazing Zoe defeats the germie germlins / Valene Campbell.

Description: Hackettstown, NJ : Woolcock Patton, 2020. | Includes 26 color

illustrations. | Series: The Amazing Zoe's Adventures ; 1. | Audience: Ages 3-9. | Summary: Zoe learns an important lesson about health and hygiene, while also finding a way to cope with coronavirus-related anxiety.

Identifiers: LCCN 2020907178 | ISBN 9781777189501 (hardback) |

ISBN 9781777189518 (pbk.) | ISBN 9781777189525 (epub)

Subjects: LCSH: Children -- Health and hygiene -- Juvenile literature. |

Coronavirus infections -- Prevention -- Juvenile literature. | Hand washing -- Juvenile literature. | Space -- Social aspects -- Juvenile literature.| BISAC: JUVENILE FICTION / Health & Daily Living / Daily Activities. |JUVENILE FICTION / Health & Daily Living / Diseases, Illnesses & Injuries.

Classification: LCC PZ7.1 C36 Am 2020 | [E]--dc22

LC record available at https://lccn.loc.gov/2020907178

The Amazing Zoe
Defeats The Germie Germlins

Written by
Valene Campbell

Germie Germlins lived on a planet far away called Virion. They were tiny monsters that were mean and nasty. Germie Germlins became happier and grew in number when they had a chance to touch anyone or any living thing. Germie Germlins would make people, animals or even trees very sick.

One day, Gerry Germlin, the Germlins' chief, gathered all the Germlins of Virion together to tell them some BIG news. He said, "I have an idea. Let's make more of us. We will visit the humans and live amongst them. We will become stronger and then take over the planet Earth and even the entire galaxy!"

The Germie Germlins cheered with excitement. "YAY!!" they shouted, and jumped in their trusted spaceship called AMINO and made their way to Planet Earth.

The next day, little Zoe was on her way home from school. She hopped off the school bus but didn't see her mom standing at the front door, waiting to greet her as she did every day. "Hmmm, I wonder where my mommy is," said Zoe.

Zoe saw a note taped to the front door. It read:
"Hi Zoe, come inside; I left a cheese sandwich and a glass of
milk on the kitchen table. I am in bed, I don't feel so well. ~MOMMY"

After going inside, Zoe ate her sandwich, drank her glass of milk, and went upstairs to see her mommy lying in bed.

When Zoe got to her parents' bedroom, she asked, "Mommy, what's wrong? I didn't see you when I hopped off the school bus." Zoe's mommy replied,
"Mommy has a stuffy nose and...Ah...Ah....AHCHOOOOO! I feel aches and pains all over."

"Oh, no!" Zoe said. "Don't worry Mommy, I'll play quietly until Daddy gets home."
"That's my good girl," replied Zoe's mommy.

The next day, Zoe went off to school and noticed her teacher wasn't in class.
"Where is Mr. Periwinkle?" asked Zoe. The supply teacher, Ms. Rosewater, said, "Mr. Periwinkle is home with the flu, I will be here for you and the class until he feels better." Zoe continued to do her class work but was feeling puzzled.

After school, Zoe went home, and when she got to her front door, she noticed a new mail lady delivering the mail. "Hello," Zoe said to the mail lady, "where is Mrs. Post, our usual mail lady?"

"Mrs. Post is home with the flu, I will deliver your mail until she feels better," replied the new mail lady.

Zoe became sad. She couldn't understand why so many people she loved and cared for were feeling sick.

Later that day, Mayor Bluebottom called all of the people together from Niceville to tell them something important. He told the people that they have been invaded by tiny germie monsters called Germlins and that they were up to no good by making everyone sick with the flu. He said one way we can beat them is to 'Stay At Home' until we can figure out how to defeat them for good. This means:

Zoe was worried. She asked Mayor Bluebottom, "what will become of our summer? Will we have to stay inside the entire time?"..... Mayor Bluebottom replied, "the sooner we defeat them, the sooner we can get back to doing everything we like to do. But until then, staying at home is all we can do for now."

The entire town became very upset, and so did Zoe. What was the summer with no swimming pools, no parks, or even going out for ice cream? She knew she had to do something!

Gerry Germlin sent billions, trillions, and gazillions of Germlins all over the world. Day to day, people were getting sore throats, stuffy noses, aches, and pains. There was no sign of the people of Niceville being able to leave their houses or have the summer that they were looking forward to.

One day, Gerry Germlin, with many of his friends, came to Zoe's very own home. Unsuspecting that the Germlins were hiding in the kitchen, Zoe had just come out of the bathroom while drying her hands. Suddenly, they all came face to face.

They attempted to jump on Zoe's hands and clothes, but suddenly, she was protected by a magical forcefield. The Germlins couldn't get to her. Standing tall, she told them that she wasn't afraid. The Germlins began to slightly shrivel, became a little smaller, and then dashed through the door. While racing away, Gerry Germlin shouted over his shoulder that they would be back!

Zoe was relieved that the Germie Germlins left without making her sick, but she couldn't figure out why?

"I know!" said Zoe. "Maybe it was the broccoli that was left on the counter top. I'm going to leave it right here until they return."

The next day, fewer of the Germlins returned while Zoe was washing the jelly stain out of Teddy's arm. The Germlins attempted to touch Zoe's hands, but Zoe was protected once again by the magical forcefield. The Germlins started to shrivel even more, turned around, and ran out of Zoe's house. Gerry Germlin shouted angrily, "WE'LL BE BACK!" Zoe closed the door behind them once they left.

Zoe thought to herself, hmmm, maybe the Germie Germlins are afraid of Teddy? So she decided to leave Teddy on the kitchen counter overnight.

The next day, Gerry Germlin and his friends came back again! This time, Zoe had just come out of the bath. Gerry Germlin was furious! He shouted, "Ugh! Every time we have come to your house, you have been washing your hands with soap and water. We like dirt and germs! We don't like anything clean! We're never coming back to this house again! Let's find someone else to jump on so we can regain our strength," Gerry Germlin said to the other Germlins.

It was at that moment Zoe knew what she had to do. She needed to tell Mayor Bluebottom and all the people of Niceville what she had learned.

Zoe ran over to Mayor Bluebottom's house. "Mayor Bluebottom, Mayor Bluebottom, we can defeat the Germie Germlins by washing our hands with soap and water!

We need to wash our hands for at least 20 seconds on all sides and in between our fingers to make it really work. It's also important that we wash our hands often throughout the day. We have to tell the people of Niceville!"

Mayor Bluebottom went on Quickgram to warn the people of Niceville and the rest of the world. Once the entire town started to wash their hands, a forcefield was created over everyone! This made the Germie Germlins weaker and weaker, and

they became fewer in number. Gerry Germlin shouted in a loud voice to the remaining Germie Germlins, "RETREAT! RETREAT! The people of Niceville have found our secret weakness. We must return to Virion and never come back to Earth."

Once the Germie Germlins returned home, everyone in Niceville started to feel much better. No more sneezing. No more stuffy noses. No more body aches.

The next day, Zoe was happy to see that everything went back to normal. It was the last day of school, and Zoe's favourite teacher, Mr. Periwinkle, was back in the classroom.

Mrs. Post returned to delivering the mail,

and Zoe's mommy was feeling much better. Zoe's mommy picked Zoe up at the bus stop and they went for ice cream to celebrate the beginning of summer.

CPSIA information can be obtained
at www.ICGtesting.com
Printed in the USA
BVHW022139050921
615964BV00001BA/3

9 781777 189501